ASLEEP, ASLEEP

BY MIRRA GINSBURG

INSPIRED BY A VERSE OF A. VVEDENSKY

ILLUSTRATED BY NANCY TAFURI

GREENWILLOW BOOKS · NEW YORK

Are the wolves asleep?
Asleep.

And the bees?
Asleep.

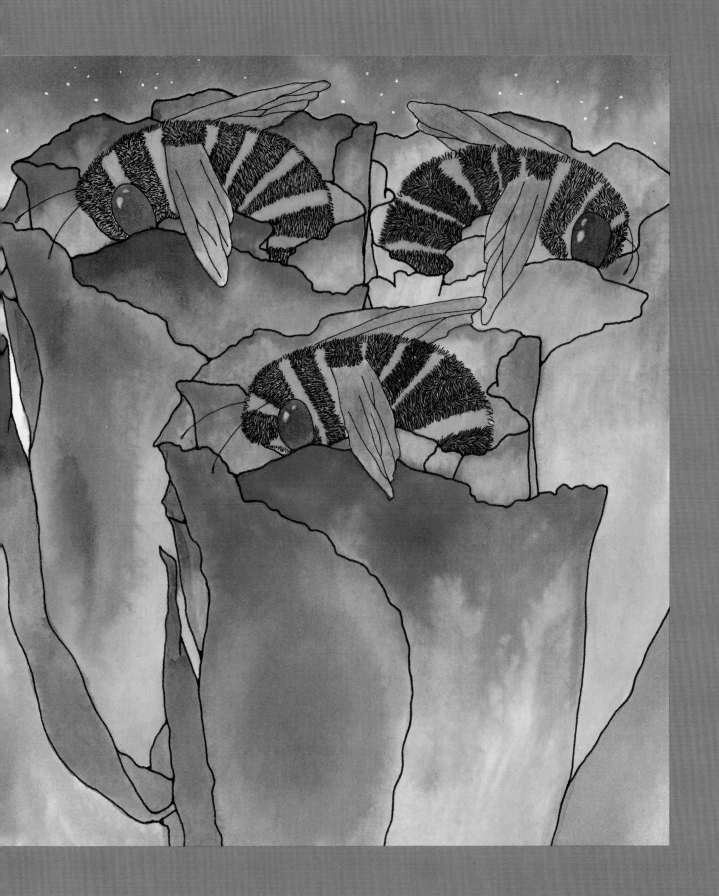

And the birds?
Asleep, asleep.

And the foxes?
Fast asleep.

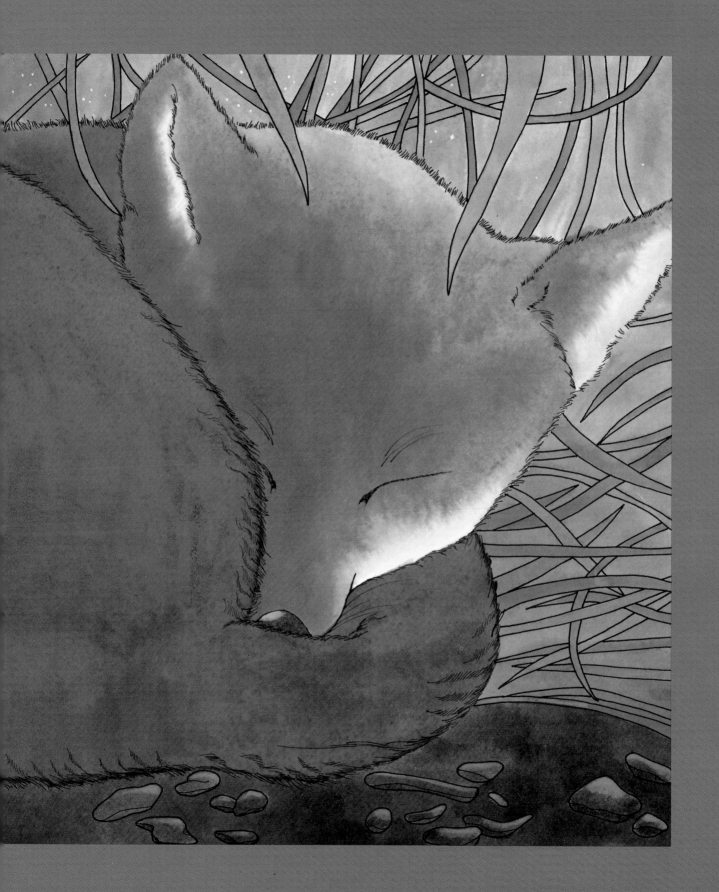

And the squirrels?
Asleep.

And the fish in the deep?
Asleep, asleep.

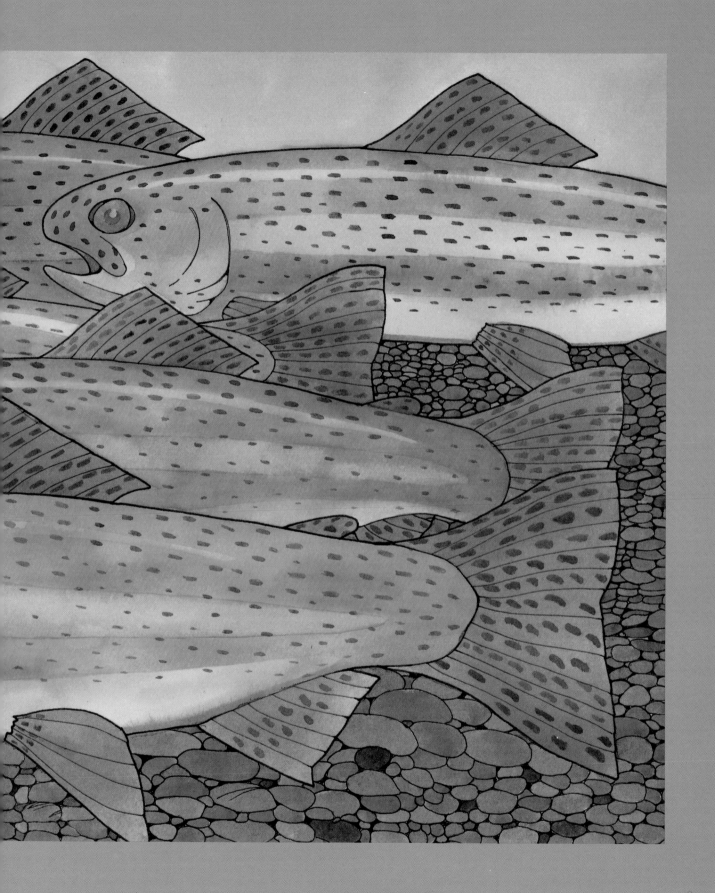

And the children?
All asleep.

Everything and everyone,
Asleep, asleep.
Only you and the wind
Are awake.

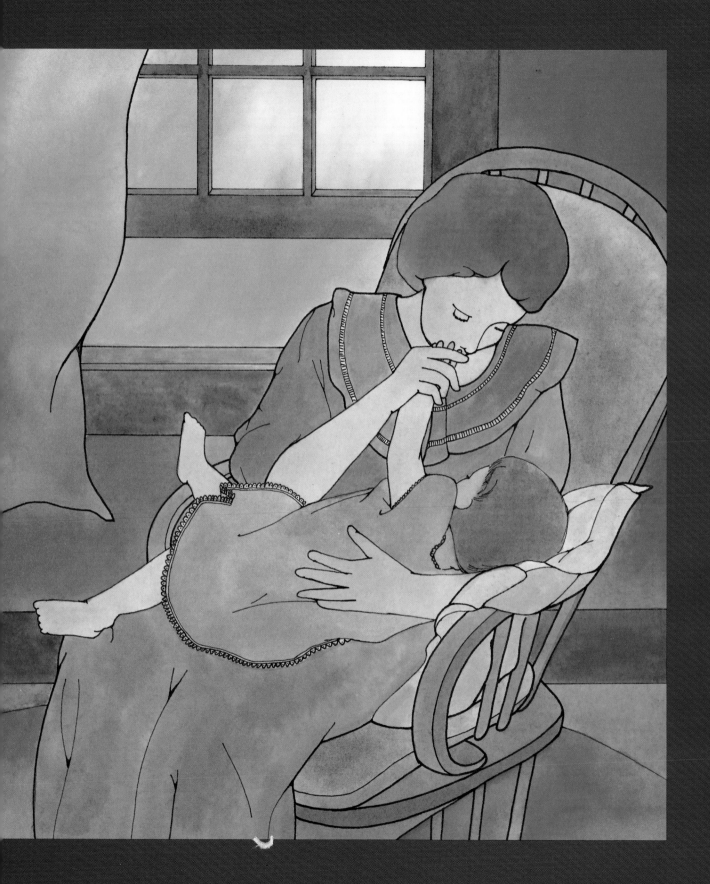

Everything and everyone,
Sleep, sleep, sleep."

TO
HELENA, RANDY,
AND JUSTIN
—M. G.

FOR CRISTINA
—N. T.

Library of Congress Cataloging-in-Publication Data

Ginsburg, Mirra.
Asleep, asleep/by Mirra Ginsburg;
pictures by Nancy Tafuri.
p.   cm.
Summary: Everything everywhere is asleep except
for the wind and one wakeful child.
ISBN 0-688-09153-9 (trade).
ISBN 0-688-09154-7 (lib.)
[1. Sleep—Fiction.]   I. Tafuri, Nancy, ill.
II. Title.   PZ7.G43896As   1992
[E]—dc20   91-14383   CIP   AC

Watercolor inks and a
black pen were used
for the full-color art.
The text type
is Leamington.

Text copyright © 1992
by Mirra Ginsburg
Illustrations copyright
© 1992 by Nancy Tafuri

Printed in Hong Kong
by South China Printing
Company (1988) Ltd.
First Edition
10 9 8 7 6 5 4 3 2 1